Made with Love

Written by Susie Linn

Illustrated by Sally Garland

TOP THAT

Licensed exclusively to Top That Publishing Ltd
Tide Mill Way, Woodbridge, Suffolk, IP12 1AP, UK
www.topthatpublishing.com
Copyright © 2017 Tide Mill Media
All rights reserved
0 2 4 6 8 9 7 5 3 1
Manufactured in China

ISBN 978-1-78700-499-3

A catalogue record for this book is available from the British Library

Every Monday, Wednesday and Friday,
Maisy went to Grandma's house.

Maisy and Grandma always had such fun together,
but today was extra special. It was Maisy's birthday!

'We're going to make a birthday cake,' said Grandma,
giving Maisy a big hug. 'And we're going to use a
very special recipe … an old one that my grandma
used for my birthday cakes.'

'What's in the cake?' asked Maisy, as they went into the kitchen.

Grandma thought for a minute. 'It's made with love.'

'Made with love?' said Maisy, looking puzzled.

'You'll see,' said Grandma, getting out the mixing bowls, spoons and cake tins.

Grandma and Maisy put on their aprons. Then Grandma opened the kitchen cupboard and took out bags, boxes and tiny bottles.

Maisy climbed onto a stool to get a better look. 'What's in these?' she asked, as Grandma put everything on the table.

'Ah!' said Grandma, winking. 'These are the secret ingredients!'

'What do we do first?' asked Maisy.

'We need to start with some kindness,' said Grandma, putting a lump of something into a big mixing bowl.

'Kindness?' said Maisy, surprised.

'Yes, kindness,' said Grandma, smiling. Then she weighed out something from a paper bag. 'And fun,' she said, adding it to the bowl. 'Kindness and fun go together well.'

Grandma showed Maisy how to mash and squish the kindness and fun together. Then it was Maisy's turn.

'What's next?' asked Maisy.

'Patience … we need two lots of patience,' said Grandma.

Grandma put two lots of patience into a little bowl and handed Maisy the whisk.

'Now whisk it all up, as hard as you can,' said Grandma. 'Patience needs to be light and frothy!'

When the patience was ready, Grandma showed Maisy how to stir it into the big bowl of kindness and fun.

Then Grandma weighed out the next secret ingredient.

'What is it?' said Maisy, helping her to spoon the stuff into the sieve and shake it into the mixing bowl. 'Joy,' said Grandma. 'We need lots and lots of joy!'

Grandma showed Maisy how to fold in the joy to make the cake mixture thick and velvety. Very carefully, Maisy copied Grandma, until every bit of joy was folded in.

'We need one more thing to make the cake extra tasty,'
said Grandma, looking at the secret ingredients.
'We need a big drop of delight!'

'Is it this one?' said Maisy,
holding up one of the
little bottles.

'No, that one,' said Grandma, pointing to another bottle.

Maisy unscrewed the lid, held the bottle over the mixing bowl and let a big drop of delight plop into the cake mixture.

'Mmm, delight smells yummy!'
said Maisy, stirring it in.

At last, the birthday cake mixture was ready.
The bowl was full and heavy, so Grandma held it
while Maisy spooned the mixture into two cake tins.

Grandma put the tins in the
hot oven and set the timer.

'We've just got time to do the washing up,' said Grandma, pulling Maisy's stool over to the kitchen sink, so she could dry up.

As Maisy was drying the last spoon, the timer went off. BRRRIIIIIIING!

Maisy sniffed the puffy golden cakes. 'They smell lovely,' she said, 'but they don't look very exciting!'

'That's because they need laughter and happiness!' said Grandma.

Grandma showed Maisy how to spread a thick layer of happiness on top of one cake ...

… and how to whisk the laughter in a big bowl, until it looked like snowy mountain tops.

Finally, they spooned the laughter over the happiness and placed the second cake on top.

'All birthday cakes need a pretty topping,' said Grandma, 'and friendship makes the best!'

Grandma showed Maisy how to mix in a little water to make the friendship into a silky-smooth paste. Then they each mixed in a big drop of affection before carefully spreading the pretty topping on the cake.

'It's time for the most special secret ingredient of all,' said Grandma, picking up a little pot.

'We need a big sprinkling of love!'

Grandma took an old box
out of her kitchen cupboard.
Inside were a yellow ribbon,
four birthday candles
and a cardboard tag.

The tag had
old-fashioned
curly writing on it.
'What does it
say, Grandma?'
asked Maisy.

Made with love

Grandma smiled as she finished putting the decorations on the cake and tied on the tag.

'Made with love,' said Grandma, giving her granddaughter a big hug.

Made with love

Many, many, many years later, when Maisy was a grandma with a granddaughter of her own, her granddaughter came to stay on her birthday.

'What shall we do today, Grandma?' the little girl asked.

'We're going to make a birthday cake!' said Grandma Maisy.

'What's in it?' asked her granddaughter.

Can you guess the secret recipe?